Night of the Slime Creature

by Jennifer Eyen

illustrated by
Don Robinson

Luke
Please get done
after weekend
mom

To my brother, Jay—
who was never, ever nasty

Published by Willowisp Press, Inc.
401 E. Wilson Bridge Road, Worthington, Ohio 43085

Copyright ©1990 by Willowisp Press, Inc.

Printed in the United States of America

10 9 8 7 6 5 4 3 2 1

ISBN 0-87406-514-3

Contents

1

My Nasty Brother

I've got this little brother. A NASTY little brother. In fact, he's probably the grossest, grimiest, most disgusting little brother in the whole world. He's five years old and he is a major pain in the neck. Or maybe I should say pain in the mouth.

You see, his name is Ralph, but I call him Mouth. Ralph the Mouth.

The funny thing is, he doesn't seem to mind when I call him Mouth. I think he might even like it! Every time I call him Mouth, Ralph just laughs. Then he stretches open his huge mouth as far as it will go. He can open his mouth so wide that I can actually count all of his little white pointed teeth!

Ralph—I mean Mouth—especially likes to stretch open his mouth when there's food in it! Sometimes, big slobbery globs of food fall right out onto his shirt! And sometimes, big slobbery globs fall out on anyone who happens to be standing near him—like me!

Mouth really loves bananas. He likes to mash them up in his cheeks, then squirt them through his teeth.

"You're disgusting!" I always yell at him when he spits bananas. But when he hears me yelling, he only laughs and stretches that humongous mouth of his even wider. And out comes the food. The little weirdo ruins a lot of shirts that way!

In the summertime, Mom doesn't even let Mouth wear shirts. He runs around all day in his shorts and sneakers. In the evening, Mom just hoses him down before he goes to bed! Now, let me tell you, that's gross!

There's only one place where I'm safe

from Mouth and his gross habits. And that's in my room. Mouth is never allowed in my room, never ever. Even Mom and Dad knock before they come in. It's where I keep all my special stuff.

But of all the things in my room, there's one thing that is a hundred times better than anything else. That's my prized possession—my super-duper, silver-and-black, high-powered telescope!

It has its own special cover and sits by my window on its own stand. It's really powerful. It can make the moon look like it's right across the street. But the best thing about it is that no one—and I mean no one—can touch it without asking me first. And the one person who definitely can't touch it is the weird and disgusting Ralph the Mouth!

By the way, my name is Greg. That's short for Gregory. I'm a third grader. My best friend's name is Luke. He understands my problems with the Mouth. Luke's got his own problems with his older sister. She's fourteen and almost as big a pain in the neck as Mouth. Her name is Roderica, but we call her Ratface. Luke thought it up. He's got a lot of style.

Anyway, Luke can tell you that everything I'm about to say is absolutely true! It didn't start out to be scary, but it sure turned out that way!

2

Disaster Strikes!

It all started one Saturday afternoon.

I was taking the cover off my telescope. I wanted to set it up to look at the planet Venus that night. Then I heard a knock at my bedroom door.

"Get lost, Mouth!" I yelled. Mouth was always trying to get into my room.

"It's me—Luke."

I opened the door.

"Hi, Luke! Come on in," I said.

"What are you doing?" Luke asked.
But before I could answer, someone else
knocked. "Who is it?" I yelled.

"It's me! It's me!" a creepy little voice
yelled back.

14

Luke and I looked at each other and said at the same time, "Mouth!"

"Go away, Mouth!" I yelled again.

"Can I come into your room?" he begged.

"No way! Get lost, Mouth."

There was silence for a moment. "Help! Help!" Mouth started to shout. Luke and I just shook our heads.

"Help me! Help me!" Mouth shouted again. "There's a...a...big bug in my hair and I can't get it out! Help me, Greg!"

"He is so weird," I sighed.

"Maybe you'd better open the door," said Luke.

"Okay," I said. And I opened the door just a crack to see what Mouth was up to.

"Look, look!" he yelled, pointing to the top of his head. "Get the bug, Greg!"

I looked at Mouth's head and saw a big, black, gooey raisin sticking out of his hair.

Luke started to laugh. I said to Mouth, "It's not a bug. It's a raisin!"

"Oh," said Mouth. And he reached up, snatched the raisin from his hair, and popped it into his mouth. Gross!

"Can I come in?" he asked again as he chewed on the raisin.

"I said, no!"

"Why not?" he started to whine.

"Because we're doing stuff," I answered. "Secret stuff."

I knew that was the wrong thing to say because his eyes got really big.

"Leave us alone!" I shouted. I slammed the door shut.

"Are you going to use your telescope tonight?" asked Luke.

"Yeah," I said, taking off its cover. "Tonight the skies are going to be clear and I should be able to see Venus really well in the telescope."

We set the telescope up and then we went over to the park to shoot some baskets before dinner.

I knew something was wrong the minute we got back from the park. The door to my room was open and I never leave that door open. When Luke and I looked in, I couldn't believe my eyes!

My most favorite thing, my silver-and-black, super-duper, high-powered telescope was in pieces all over my bedroom floor!

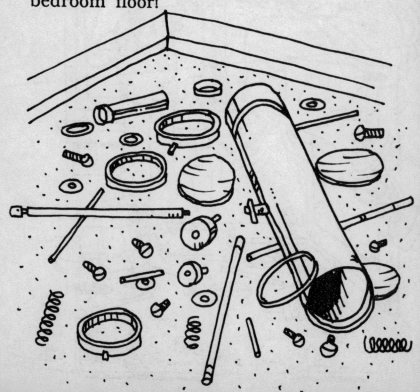

3

This Means WAR!

"Arrrrgh! My telescope! My telescope!" I screamed. I jumped around my room. I kicked my bed.

"What could have happened?" Luke asked.

"I can't believe it!" I kept yelling. "It's in pieces!"

"Uh-oh. Look at this," Luke said, holding up a lens. There was a big, gooey raisin stuck to it.

"I'm going to murder that Mouth!" I yelled.

Mom and Dad heard the shouting and came in to see what was the matter.

"What happened?" Dad asked.

"When we got back from the park, this is how we found my telescope," I explained.

Mom and Dad looked at each other. Then they both shouted at the same time, "Ralph! Where are you?"

They were the only ones who called him Ralph. Mouth poked his head in the door. He never looked up.

"Ralph, do you know anything about this?" asked Mom, pointing at my telescope.

"I'm sorry," Mouth answered. "I only wanted to see Venus."

"What do you mean, Ralph?" Dad asked.

"Well," Mouth began, "I heard Greg tell Luke that he was going to look at Venus in the telescope. I wanted to see Venus, too."

"You were listening at the door, you little sneak!" I screamed.

"When they went to the park, I came in here and looked in the telescope to

see Venus. But I couldn't find it. So, I unscrewed that thing on the end of it to look inside better. I knew Venus must be in there somewhere. I just kept taking pieces off to look inside better."

"You idiot!" I yelled. "Venus is a planet! It's up in the sky! It's not IN the telescope. You look at Venus in the sky WITH the telescope! I think I'm going to faint!"

"No one's going to faint," Dad said. "But someone's going to be punished for doing something bad."

"Sell him, Dad!" I said. "Just sell Mouth and we can use the money to pay someone to put my telescope back together again!"

"We're not selling your brother," Mom said, shaking her head. "But Ralph can't watch TV for two weeks."

"Two whole weeks?" asked Mouth with a frown.

"What?!?!" I screamed. "That's it? That's all you're going to do to him?"

I couldn't believe it. Mouth deserved

a lot worse than two weeks without TV. I decided then and there I would have to get revenge on my brother. I was declaring war on Mouth!

"Why don't you go over to Luke's house for a couple of hours," said Dad. "Ralph and I will clean up this mess while you're gone, won't we, Ralph? I think I might be able to fix the telescope."

But Mouth didn't have much to say. It was about the only time I ever saw his mouth closed!

4

REVENGE!

Luke and I walked to his house. We had to find a way to get even with Mouth. When we got to Luke's house, we heard a weird, awful noise.

"What's that noise?" I asked Luke. "Is someone scratching their fingernails down a blackboard?"

29

"No."

"Are three dogs and two cats having a big fight in your living room?"

"No, that's only Ratface singing," he answered. Sure enough, Roderica—I mean Ratface—was sitting on her bed, singing along to her favorite tape while she polished her toenails.

"Watch this," whispered Luke. He got

down on the floor and quietly crawled into Ratface's room. She was so busy singing, that she didn't even notice him crawl under her bed.

He looked back at me for a second, grinning. Then he grabbed her ankle and screamed as loud as he could!

"AARRRGGGHHHH!!!"

Ratface was so frightened that her hands flew up in the air. So did the bottle of bright red nail polish. The bottle landed right in her lap, spilling all over her shirt!

Boy, I've never seen Ratface so angry! She grabbed for Luke, but he jumped up and yelled to me, "Run! Run!"

We ran into Luke's room and locked the door just before Ratface could get us.

"I'll get you for this, you little twerp!" she yelled at the door.

"Sisters!" said Luke. "What a pain in the neck."

"They're as bad as brothers," I said. Now let's think of a way to get even with Mouth. This is war!"

"Right," said Luke. "Let's give him a good scare, like we just did to Ratface!"

"Yeah. But one big scare's not enough. It has to be better than that," I answered. "It has to be...terrifying."

We sat and thought for a long time, until I began to get an idea. A horrible, terrible, fabulous, fantastic idea. A green, scaly, slobbering, sharp-toothed, long-clawed, bulgy-eyed, slime-spitting idea!

For the rest of the evening, Luke and

I sat in his room, creating...the SLIME CREATURE!

5

Hello, Slime Creature?

Luke and I couldn't wait to tell Mouth about the Slime Creature. We went back over to my house and asked Mouth if he'd like for us to tell him a story before bed.

He looked a little surprised because he knew I was still mad at him. But he also liked stories. So Mouth, Luke, and I sat down and we began to tell him a little bedtime story about the terrible Slime Creature!

"What does it look like?" Mouth asked with big eyes.

"It's horrible!" I explained. "It's the ugliest creature in the world. It's all green and has little crispy scales all over its body. It's got big, bulging, watery eyes. It has long, razor-sharp claws. It has huge teeth that have sticky clumps of hair caught between them from chewing the heads off of little brothers. Worst of all, it spits terrible green slime at its victims that paralyzes them so they can't run away!"

By this time, Mouth was looking a little pale.

"Where does the Slime Creature live?" Mouth asked softly. Luke and I looked at each other.

"Well," I began, "he lives right here in our town."

"In OUR town?" Mouth shouted, jumping to his feet. "Oh, no!"

Right then we knew our plan was going to be a success. Mouth believed everything. You should have seen his

face when we told him that we knew the Slime Creature's telephone number!

The next day after school I was watching a movie on TV. Just to test Mouth, I asked him to get me some potato chips from the kitchen.

"Get them yourself," he said, sticking out his tongue.

"Okay," I sighed. "I guess I'll just have to call the Slime Creature and tell him to come over here and chew your head off."

I stood up and walked to the phone. As I dialed, Mouth's eyes got bigger and bigger. I thought they were going to pop out of his head when I said, "Hello, Slime Creature? This is Greg."

Mouth jumped up and ran to the kitchen yelling, "I'll get your chips, I'll get your chips!"

Of course, he didn't know that I just called the number that gives you the weather report.

Everything was going great until something really strange happened.

On Wednesday when I got home from

school, there was a letter waiting for me. I hardly ever get letters, so I opened it up right away. It said:

Dear Greg,

If you don't stop picking on Mouth, I'm coming over to your house to chew YOUR head off!

The Slime Creature

6

A Mysterious Letter

A letter from the Slime Creature? I couldn't believe my eyes!

I called Luke on the phone and told him to come over to my house right away. When he got to my house, I showed him the letter.

"I don't get it," Luke said. "How can this be from the Slime Creature? We made up the Slime Creature!"

"I know we did," I said. "This must be some kind of joke."

"Hey, wait a minute!" Luke said.

"Maybe Mouth wrote this so we wouldn't tease him anymore."

I shook my head. "First of all," I said, "I don't think Mouth knows we're teasing him. He really believes in the Slime Creature. And anyway, Mouth doesn't know how to write."

All of a sudden, Luke started to laugh. He punched me in the arm. "Okay, the joke's over, Greg," he said.

"What do you mean?" I asked.

"You really wrote this, didn't you? This is one of your crazy jokes, right?" Luke asked, still smiling.

"No way, Luke! I didn't write this. Honest. I sort of thought maybe it was YOU who was playing a joke on me!"

Luke got serious. "Honest, Greg, I did not write this note."

I knew he was telling the truth.

"But Luke, if you didn't write it, and I didn't write it, then who—"

Just then Mom came into the living room. "Oh, Greg, someone called for you on the phone while you were at school.

"Who was it?" I asked.

"I'm not sure," Mom answered. "The voice just said to tell you that he called. And when I asked who was calling, the name sounded something like...Slime Creature."

"No way!" I shouted. Luke and I gulped. The Slime Creature called my house? What was going on?

"I thought that seemed like a strange name," said Mom. "Is it some kind of joke?"

"Uh, yeah, that's right, Mom," I said. "It's probably just a joke."

When Mom left the room, Luke looked at me and said, "Greg, this is getting worse and worse."

I just nodded. He was right.

* * * * *

I didn't sleep well that night. But by the next morning, I felt a lot better—until I got home from school.

Luke was with me when I checked the mail. There was another letter! This time, it was addressed to both me and Luke. I opened the letter and read out loud. It said:

Dear Greg and Luke,

Since you are both still picking on Mouth, I am coming over to see you tomorrow night. I expect both of you to be waiting for me at Greg's house. I will be coming at dinner time, and YOU are going to be the dinner!

The Slime Creature

"Oh, no!" Luke cried.

"This is too weird!" I said. "We made up this monster! It can't be real!"

That night I tossed and turned in my sleep. I had a nightmare about the Slime Creature. He looked just the way Luke and I said he did—all green and scaly with bulging eyes and ugly claws and fangs with hair in them. And when I tried to run, the Slime Creature would spit this awful green slime on me and I couldn't move!

7

Night
of the Slime Creature

The next evening, Luke came over for dinner—to eat dinner, not BE dinner. That was pretty brave of him, since a slime creature was coming over to chew his head off. But, like I said, Luke and I were best pals.

It was just starting to get dark. The wind was blowing really hard and whistling around the house. It looked like we might have a storm.

We could hear Mom fixing dinner in the kitchen. Dad was in the study reading. Luke, Mouth, and I just sat on the sofa watching the front door and listening to the wind howl outside. Mouth was just as nervous about the Slime

Creature as we were.

"It'll be a full moon tonight," I said.

"Maybe we should tell your Mom and Dad about this," Luke said.

"What should I say?" I asked Luke. "Hey, Mom and Dad. We're waiting here on the sofa for a slime creature to come and chew our heads off? That would sound pretty dumb!"

"Hmmm, I guess you're right," he agreed. "It does sound pretty crazy."

All of a sudden, the doorbell rang! We each jumped a foot!

"It's him!" whispered Mouth. "It's the Slime Creature!"

"What should we do?" whispered Luke. "Do you think it's really him?"

Then the doorbell rang again! We heard Mom call from the kitchen, "Greg, will you get the door, please?"

We were frozen to the sofa. The doorbell rang again.

"Greg!" Mom called again. "Get the door. I'm busy!"

I gulped and stood up. "Come on," I

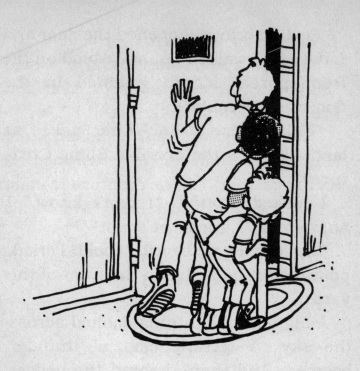

said, "we'll all go together."

So the three of us walked slowly to the door and opened it just a crack. We peeked out. It was really dark by now. We could hear thunder in the distance.

"I can't see anything," I whispered as I turned on the porch light. I opened the door a little wider and slowly stuck my head out. Still, I couldn't see anything.

Feeling braver, I opened the door and Luke and I walked out and stood on the front porch. Mouth huddled in the doorway, trembling.

"Well, where is he?" Luke asked at last. "Where's the horrible Slime Creature?"

I looked around. "I don't know," I answered. "I guess he's not—"

That's when we saw it. "Look!" I cried, pointing to the hedge in the front of the yard.

A big bolt of lightning flashed across the sky. A terrible clap of thunder boomed. And there, behind the hedge,

a figure was creeping!

"Aaarrrggghhh! There he is!" screamed Mouth. "It's the Slime Creature!!!"

Luke and I were too scared to move or speak! We just stood there on the front porch, watching in horror as the shadowy figure moved closer.

We heard a low moaning sound coming from behind the hedge. Lightning flashed again. Then, slowly, a huge green head with bulging eyes and terrible long fangs leaned out from behind the hedge.

"AAARRRGGGHHH!" all three of us screamed.

Suddenly, it seemed to see us! It stopped and stared right at us.

We were shaking in our shoes!

It raised one arm and pointed at us with a long, hideous claw.

"Greg...Luke..." it said in a horrible, growly voice. "I am the Slime Creature...and I have come to CHEW YOUR HEADS OFF!"

And then the worst thing of all happened. The Slime Creature spit out a long stream of gross, green, sticky slime right at us. It landed all over our shoes!

"AARRGHH!" Luke and I screamed. "The paralyzing slime! Run!"

We turned to run back inside the house. But Mouth had already run back inside and slammed the door shut. We couldn't get in!

8

I Love Slime!

"Help! Help!" we screamed. "Open the door! HE'S GOING TO CHEW OUR HEADS OFF!!!"

We could hear the Slime Creature's footsteps getting closer and closer. We could hear his moaning and growling. We pounded on the door.

"Greg...Luke...Greg...Luke," he kept repeating. Another gloppy stream of green slime splattered at our feet.

Just then, the door opened and we jumped inside. I locked the door.

"Mom! Dad! He's after us!" I screamed. "The Slime Creature's right outside!"

Suddenly, we realized something strange was going on. Mom, Dad, and Mouth were all standing in the hallway. They were laughing their heads off.

"W-what's so funny?" I asked. "Don't you know the Slime Creature's right outside trying to get in?"

They just kept laughing.

"I don't think we should let our visitor stay out on the porch," Dad said. "Maybe we should ask him in."

"No!" I yelled. "Don't open that door!"

But it was too late. Dad had unlocked the door and opened it wide.

There on the porch stood Ratface. She was holding a big green head from a dragon costume and a plastic bucket of something slimy and green. She was laughing so hard, she could barely stand up.

"You!" Luke and I both yelled.

Mouth walked up to her and stuck his hand into the bucket. He pulled out a handful of the slime and popped it into his mouth.

"Mmm," he said. "Lime Jell-O!"

Luke and I groaned.

Ratface said, "I heard you two planning to scare Mouth with the Slime Creature story," she said, setting the bucket of slime on the floor. "I decided to get back at you for making me spill my nail polish—and teach you a lesson about how it feels to be picked on all the time."

"So *you* wrote the letters?" Luke asked.

"That's right," she answered.

"And you called me and left a message from the Slime Creature?" I asked her.

"No," she said, shaking her head. "I never called your house. I only sent the letters."

"Huh?" I asked. "Then who called my house? Mom took the message, didn't you, Mom?"

I looked at Mom. She had a weird look on her face. "Yes, I did," she said. She looked at Roderica. "But it wasn't you, Roderica?" she asked.

Roderica shook her head. "No, it

wasn't me."

"Then I wonder who it was," Mom answered.

"I-it c-couldn't be the real Slime Creature, could it?" I asked. "I mean, we made him up. He's not real, is he?"

We were all quiet for a second, thinking about the mystery of the Slime Creature. Then Dad said, "Well, I hope you guys learned a lesson from all this."

Luke nodded. "I'm sorry I scared you, Ratf—Roderica. I won't do it again," he added.

"Well," I said. "Maybe I have been a little mean to Mouth—I mean Ralph. I'll try to be nicer to him from now on."

"That's right," said Mom. "You never know when the Slime Creature will turn up again!"

We all laughed. But I still wondered who called me up on the phone.

"Hey," said Dad, "has anybody seen Ralph?"

We all looked around. At first we couldn't see him anywhere. Then we listened and heard a sound—a disgusting, sickening sound. We all followed the sound into the living room.

There, sitting under the piano, was my little brother. He was dipping his hands into Roderica's bucket. When he

pulled them out they were covered with the green Jell-O. He was licking them clean with an awful slurping sound.

He looked up and saw us. He smiled with his huge, green mouth and gurgled, "I love slime!"

About the Author

JENNIFER EYEN started writing even before she could read. As a little girl, she used to make squiggles on paper and pretend to "read" them to her mom. Jennifer writes poetry and grown-up stuff, too. But she especially likes to write children's stories. She gets a lot of her ideas from things that really happen. When she was little, a horrible monster lived in her town. And she knew his telephone number!

Jennifer lives in Columbus, Ohio, with her husband, son, and a very silly basset hound.